MISUNDERSTOOD SHARK

Starring SHARK!

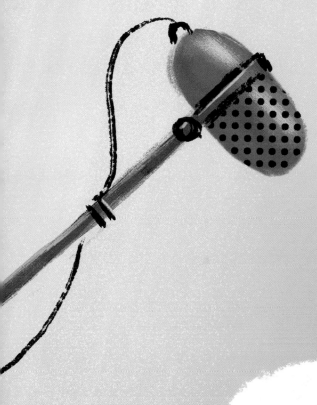

Here we go,
Underwater World with Bob
broadcasting live
in 3 . . . 2 . . .

. . . 1 . . .
Hey! Who did this?!

For Chris,
aka Big Meanie.
(But maybe he's just
misunderstood.)
—A.D.

For Owen
and Daniel.
—S.M.

ISBN
978-1-338-31589-9
• 10 9 8 7 6 5 4 3 2 1 •
18 19 20 21 22 • Printed in the
U.S.A. 169 • First printing 2018 •
The text type was set in Chelsea
Market and Adrianna Condensed.
Book design by Jess
Tice-Gilbert

MISUNDERSTOOD SHARK
Starring SHARK!

Written by Ame Dyckman

Illustrated by Scott Magoon

Scholastic Inc.

"Sharrrk!
The people are watching!
Don't eat that fish
in front of the people!"

"Showing him my new tooth!"

"Fun Fact about that! Sharks can grow and lose 30,000 teeth in their lifetime."

Can I faint now?

30,000?!

Shark's Tooth Fairy must be EXHAUSTED!

"Fine, Shark. Maybe you weren't going to eat that fish . . ."

"Shark?"

"Where's Shark?"

"I was just ..."

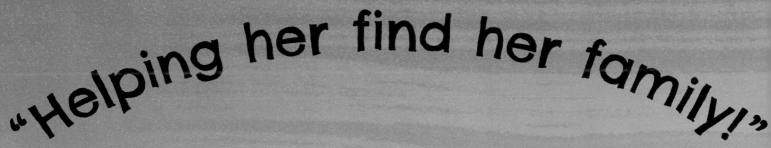

"Fun Fact about that! A great white shark can eat 22,000 pounds of food in a year . . . and seals are their favorite."

"People, I MAY have misunderstood Shark!"

"Shark?"

"Where's Shark NOW?!"

“What is it, Shark?”

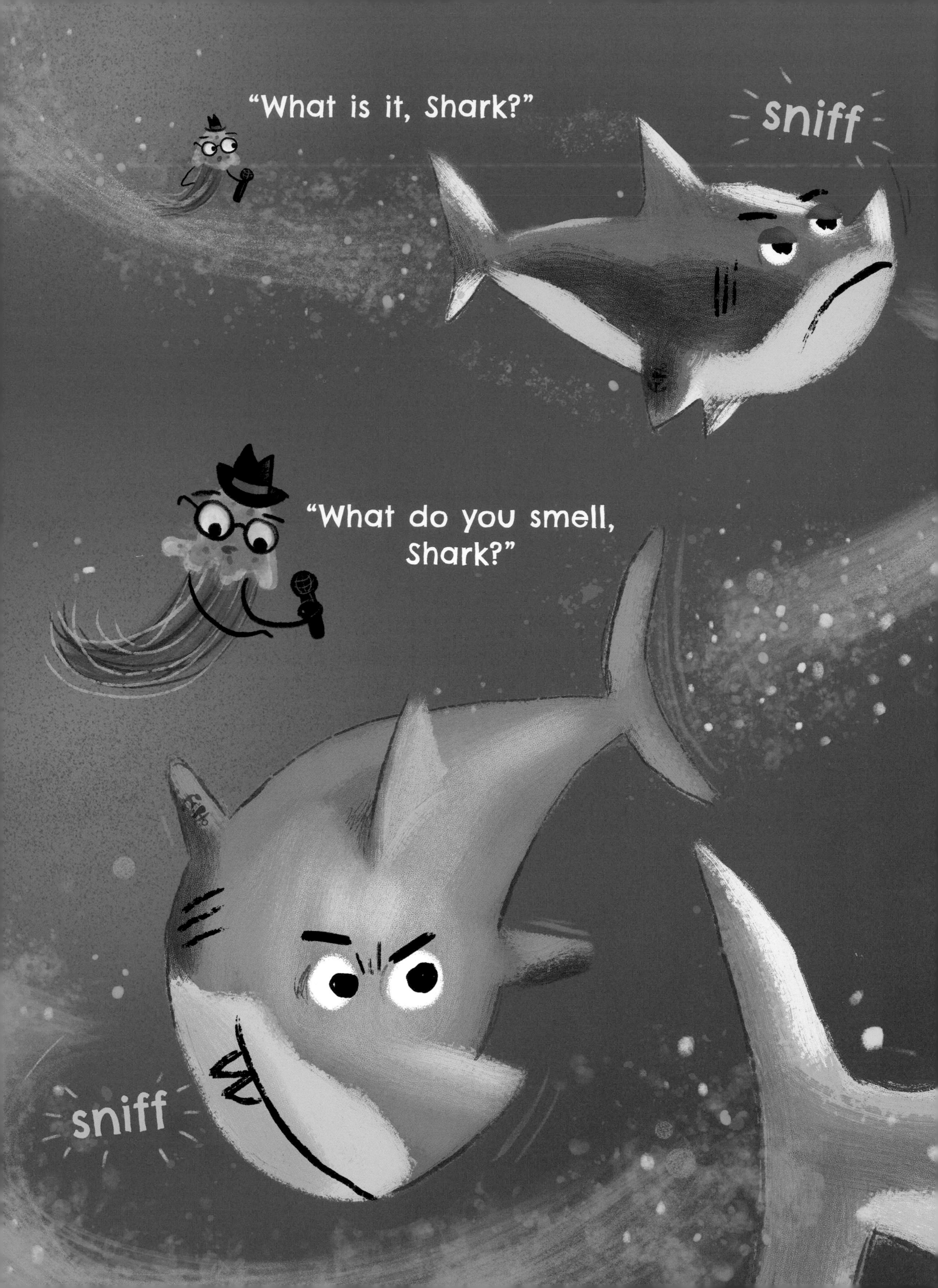

“What do you smell, Shark?”

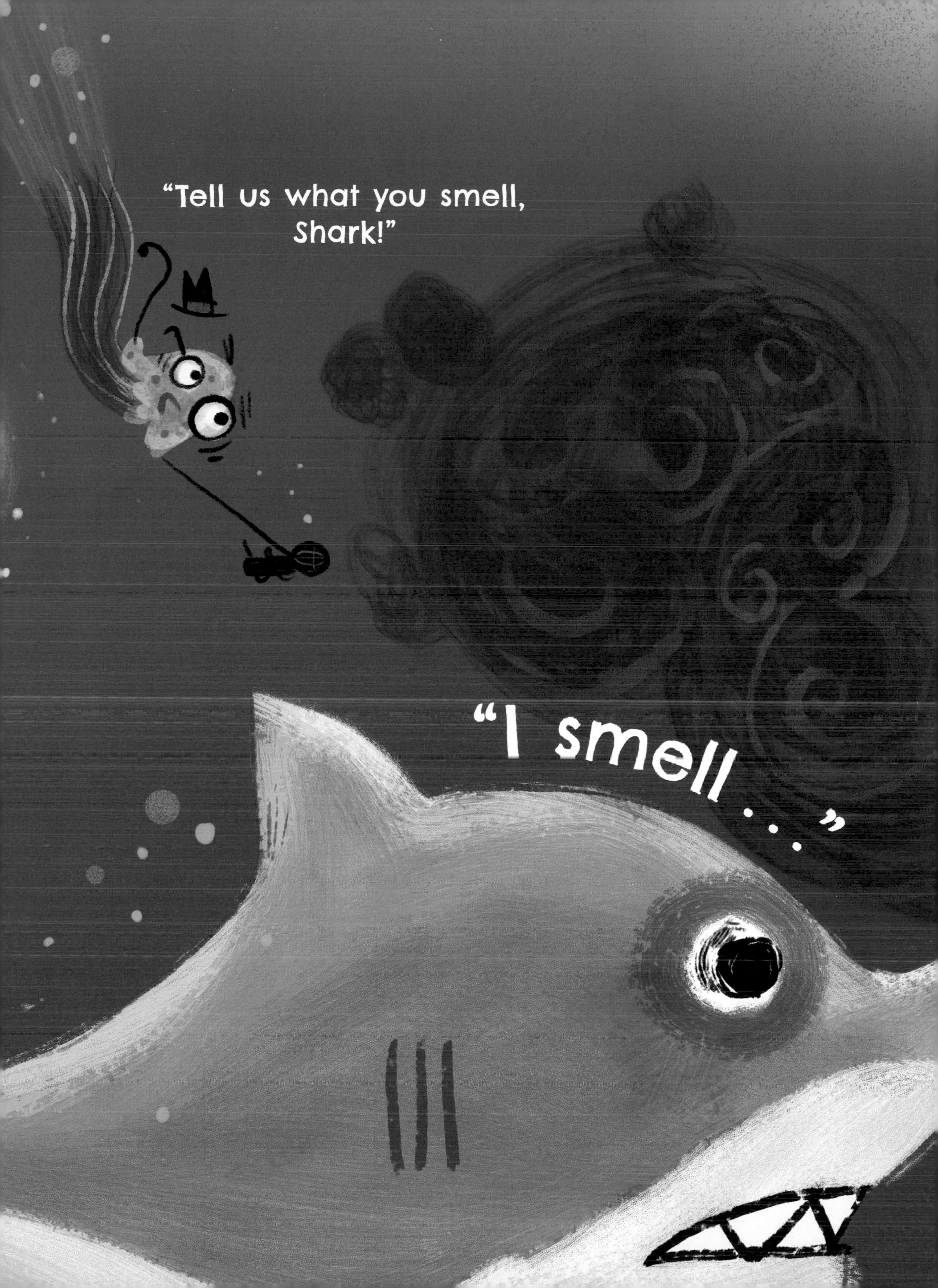
"Tell us what you smell, Shark!"
"I smell . . ."

"OH! Fun Fact about that!
Some sharks can smell
a single drop of blood
in a million drops of wa—"

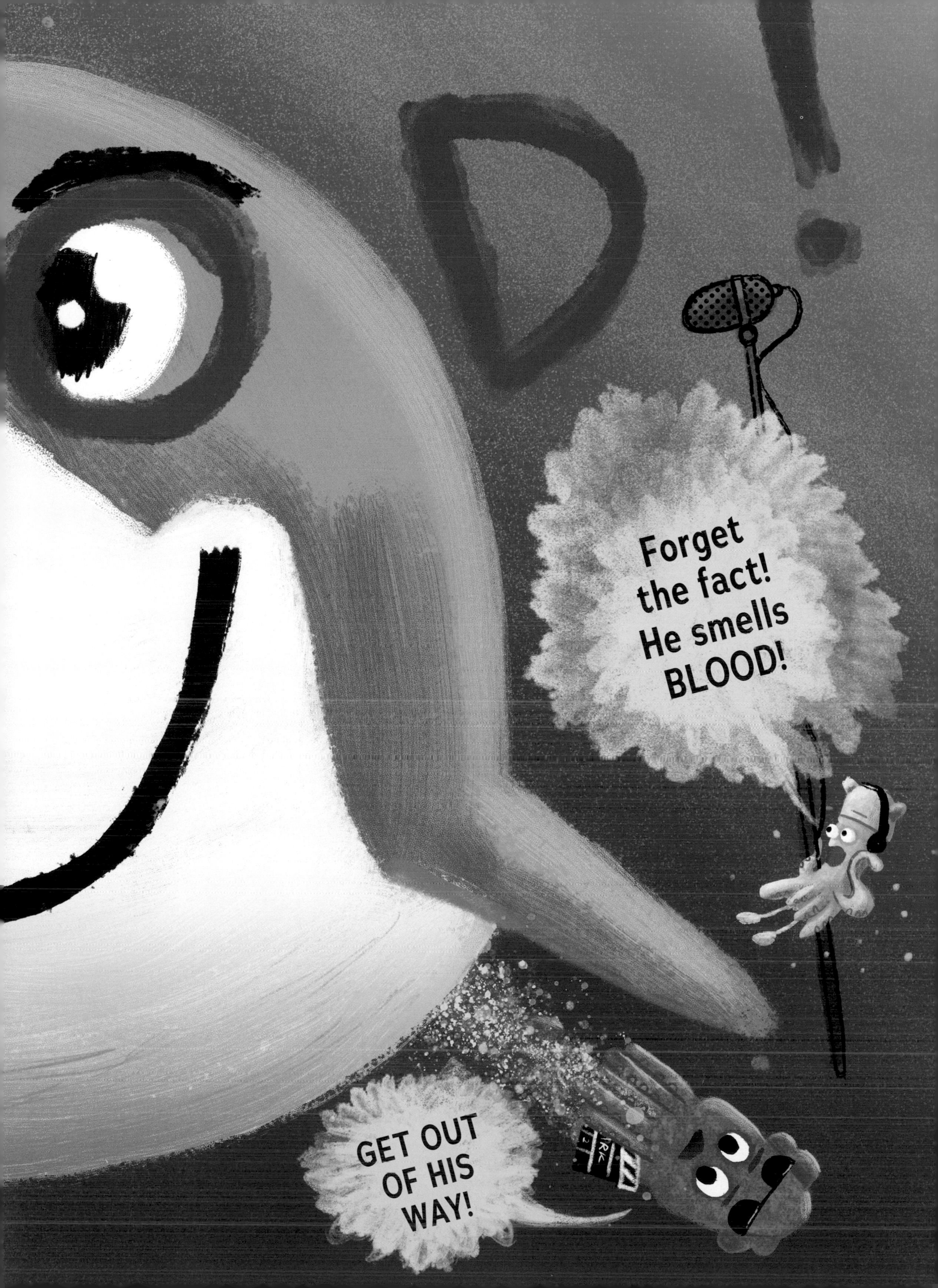
D!
Forget the fact! He smells BLOOD!
GET OUT OF HIS WAY!

"Nooo, Shark!
Don't eat the people—
IN FRONT OF THE PEOPLE!"

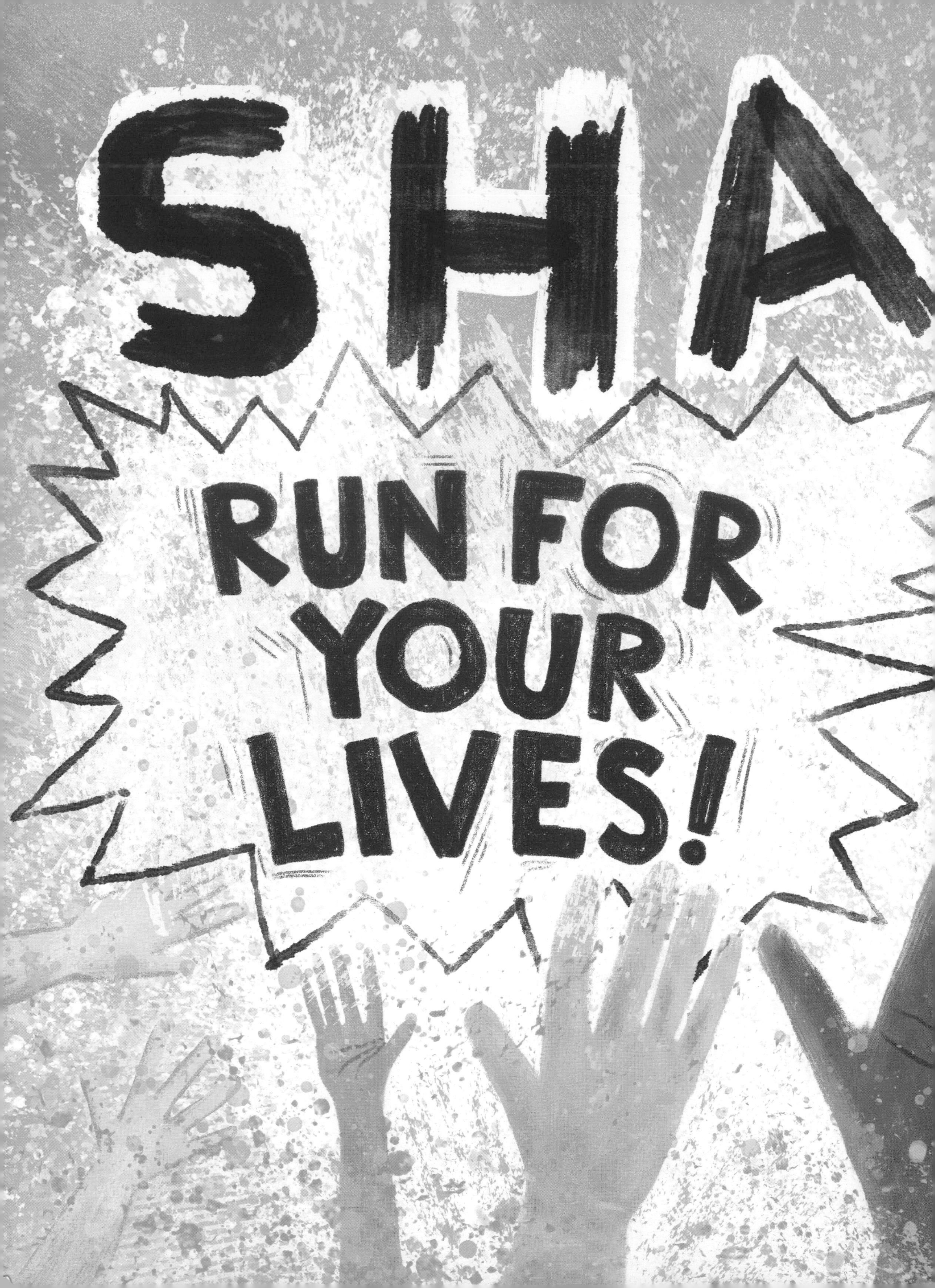
SHA
RUN FOR YOUR LIVES!

"I was just trying to help!
But the people misunderstood me, too."

"And there you have it, folks. Sharks really are . . . just misunderstood!"

GULP!
dab
dab
dab
You ate me! I can't believe you REALLY ate me!
IN FRONT OF THE PEOPLE!
SHARK

"Playing hide-and-seek with you!"

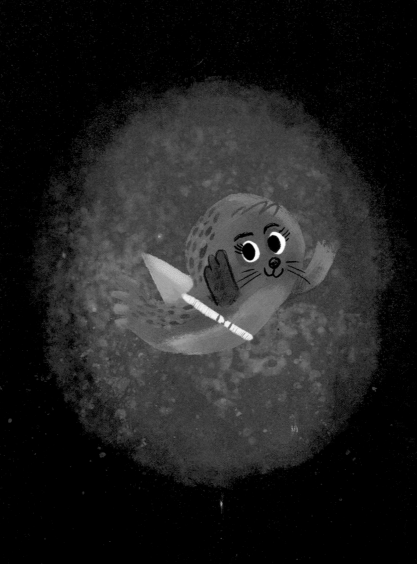